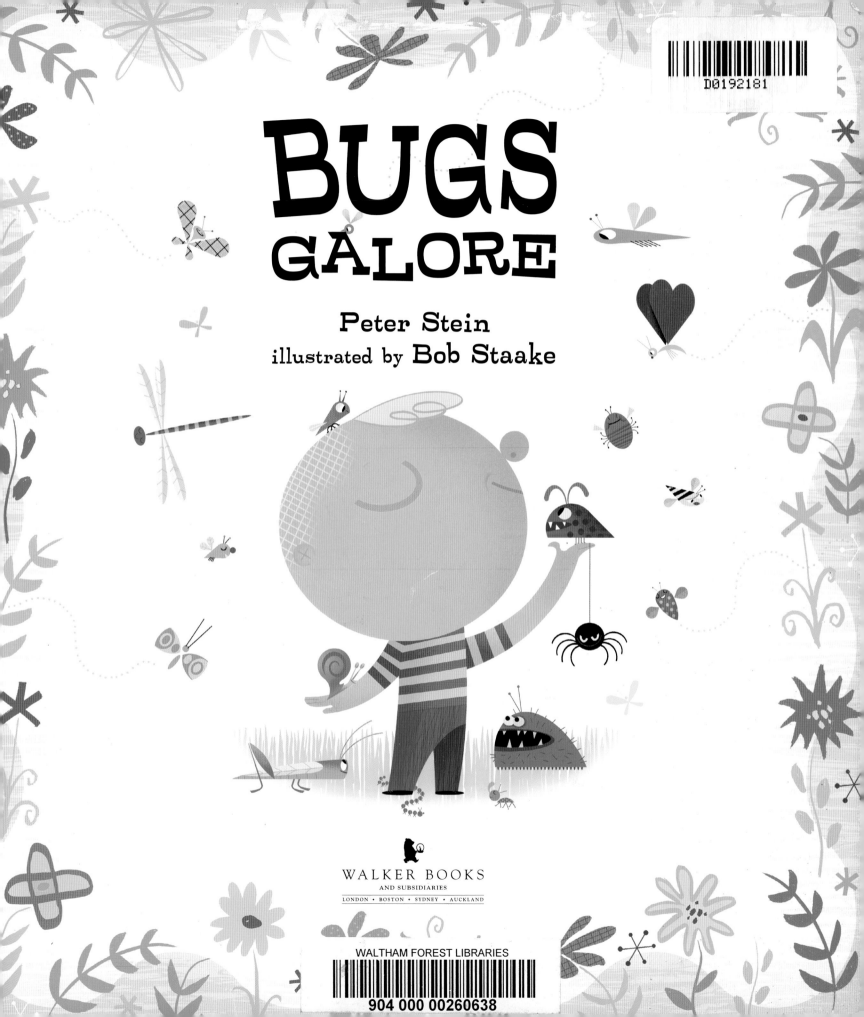

BUGS GALORE

Peter Stein

illustrated by Bob Staake

WALKER BOOKS
AND SUBSIDIARIES
LONDON · BOSTON · SYDNEY · AUCKLAND

Big bugs, small bugs,
creep bugs, crawl bugs.
Sky bugs, land bugs,
slime-your-hand bugs!

Dirt bugs, tree bugs,
hard-to-see bugs.
Mean bugs, kind bugs,
fun-to-find bugs.

Bugs and MORE bugs!
Can't ignore bugs.
Don't-inhale-them-
while-you-snore bugs!

Mud safari—
hunt for worms.
This one's squishy,
that one squirms.

Stuck-in-muck worm.
Half a YUCK worm!
Dig-down-deep-and-
find-with-luck worm.

Spider creeping . . .
scary. Gross.
Lurking . . . leaping!
Don't get close!

Freaky, sneaky,
shiny flat bug.
Hairy, scary—
what was THAT bug?

Honey-making,
buzzy bee bug.
Fuzzy, stinging,
time-to-flee bug!

Lightning glow bugs.
Nighttime show bugs.
Shining bright bugs.
What-a-sight bugs!

Some bugs cruise around in groups.
Some bugs fly in loop-de-loops.
Some bugs land smack-dab in soups.

Some bugs crawl
right under . . . OOPS.

Blah! A stinkbug!
Plug-your-nose bug!
Funky, smelly,
wash-your-clothes bug!

Bugs and bugs and billions MORE bugs! Googols, gaggles, bugs GALORE bugs!

Aaaah-bugs! Ewww-bugs!
Crawl-on-YOU bugs!
Stay away from
crawl-on-POO bugs!

Silly limb bug.
Swimming skim bug.
Frumpy plump bug.
Lumpy jump bug!

Caterpillar:
mighty changer,
body-morphing
rearranger.

Just like magic—
flapping, flailing . . .
butterfly-ing!
Soaring! Sailing!

Hurry, scurry—eating, speeding!

Hauling, sprawling—ANTS STAMPEDING!

Roly-poly,
snuggly ball bug.
Holy moly!
Ugly tall bug!

Love bugs. Shove bugs.
Head bugs. Bedbugs.
Cute bugs. Fruit bugs.
Live bugs. Dead bugs.

Bugs are awesome,
oddly mild,
feared and weird,
destructive, wild,
otherworldly,
pesky, chilling,
undercover,
fun and thrilling!

Bug, so secret,
are you wise?
Gazing out through
all those eyes?
What exactly
do you see?

I see you. . . .

Do you see me?

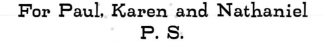

For Paul, Karen and Nathaniel
P. S.

For Giambattista Bodoni—my type of guy
B. S.

First published 2012 by Walker Books Ltd
87 Vauxhall Walk, London SE11 5HJ

This edition published 2013

2 4 6 8 10 9 7 5 3 1

This book has been typeset in Zalderdash

Printed in China

British Library Cataloguing in Publication Data:
a catalogue record for this book
is available from the British Library

ISBN 978-1-4063-4464-6

www.walker.co.uk